LITTLE SEED LITTLE SEED

Written by
Rodney Cox Jr.

Illustrated by Anthony Chitay

There once was a little seed that was eager to grow.

Rain rain I want rain because I am small rain will help me grow big and tall.

The little seed could not wait to grow.

"Maybe I will be a pretty flower or even a strong tree I cannot wait to see what I will be, but first I need it to rain."

"But first I need it to rain."
The little seed would say.

Every day the little seed grew less and less patient. Often the little seed would cry out to the farmer:

"Farmer farmer where is the rain sunny days are all the same?"

And the farmer would reply with these words of wisdom:

"little seed little seed listen to me, a lot of rain is not would you need.

A little bit of rain and a little bit of sun is how all of the growing is done."

But the little seed did not care about the farmers words. The little seed was not interested in the process it would take to grow. The little seed just wanted to grow.

"Rain rain I want rain!"
the little seed yelled out.

The little seed was so anxious for it to start raining that, the little seed missed the first few drops of the rainfall.

Drip drop drip.

"Yay rain!"

The little seed was so excited to finally see the rain.

However the little seed was overwhelmed with how much rain was coming down. "Wait wait this is too much rain! Oh no!"

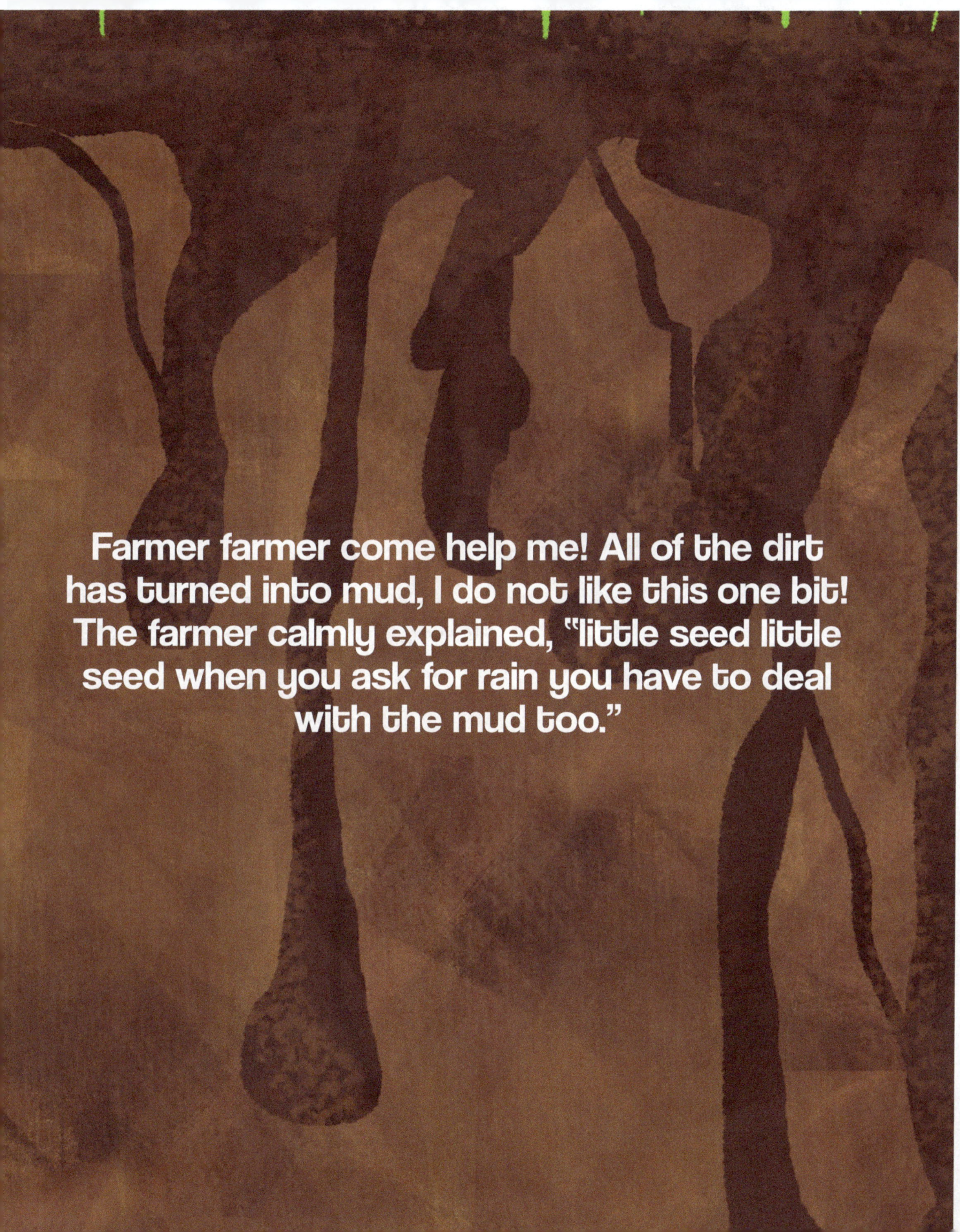

Farmer farmer come help me! All of the dirt has turned into mud, I do not like this one bit! The farmer calmly explained, "little seed little seed when you ask for rain you have to deal with the mud too."

The little seed only thought about the rain but never stopped to think about everything that comes along with the rain.

"What do I do with all this mud?"
The little seed asked the farmer. And the farmer responded,

"grow past it little seed. The sun will come out and the mud will dry so there is no need to cry."

Just as the farmer said the rain ended in the warm sun was in the sky shining once again.

"Now that the sun is back in the sky what do I do about all this mud?"
the little seed asked.

"Little seed little seed be patient I know the mud will dry. Sometimes a little growth takes a lot of time."
Said the farmer.

"Farmer farmer look at me I am a pretty flower no longer a seed."

A pretty flower indeed!